MINI CLASSICS

PINOCCHIO

RETOLD BY STEPHANIE LASLETT
ILLUSTRATED BY ANDREW GEESON

‖ •PARRAGON• ‖

TITLES IN SERIES I AND III OF THE MINI CLASSICS INCLUDE:

SERIES I

Aladdin and the Magic Lamp
Ali Baba and the Forty Thieves
Alice in Wonderland
A Child's Garden of Verses
Cinderella
The Emperor's New Clothes
The Frog Prince
Goldilocks and the Three Bears
Hansel and Grettel
The Happy Prince
The Little Mermaid
Mother Goose's Rhymes
The Owl and the Pussycat (and other Nonsense Verse)
Puss in Boots
Sleeping Beauty
Snow White and the Seven Dwarfs
The Town Mouse and the Country Mouse (and other
   Aesop's Fables)
The Three Little Pigs
The Ugly Duckling
The Wizard of Oz

SERIES III

Alice Through the Looking-Glass

Brer Rabbit's Riding Horse (and other Stories)

Brer Rabbit and the Turtle Race (and other Stories)

The Cat that Walked by Himself

The Elephant's Child (and How the Camel got his Hump)

The Fox without a Tail (and other Aesop's Fables)

The Golden Goose

Hush-a-Bye Baby (A Collection of Prayers
  and Lullabies)

The Little Match-Girl (and The Swineherd)

A Little Princess

Peter and the Wolf

Peter Pan

The Pied Piper of Hamelin

The Princess and the Pea (and The Red Shoes)

The Remarkable Rocket

Rumpelstiltskin

The Sorcerer's Apprentice

Tom Thumb

Wind in the Willows III – The Adventures of Toad

Wind in the Willows IV – Return to Toad Hall

For Sam — SL

A Parragon Book

Published by
Parragon Books,
Unit 13-17, Avonbridge Trading Estate,
Atlantic Road, Avonmouth, Bristol BS11 9QD

Produced by
The Templar Company plc,
Pippbrook Mill, London Road, Dorking, Surrey RH4 1JE

Copyright © 1994 Parragon Book Service Limited

Designed by Mark Kingsley-Monks

Printed and bound in Great Britain

ISBN 1-85813-763-2

There was once upon a time — a piece of wood! It was not a valuable piece of wood. No, it was just an ordinary log like those that are burned in stoves and fireplaces to make a cheerful blaze and warm the room. This piece of wood lay in the workshop of an old carpenter called Master Geppetto. He lived in this little room all by himself. The furniture could not have been simpler — a bad chair, a poor bed and a broken-down workbench.

As soon as he set eyes on this
piece of wood he beamed with
delight. "This wood will make
a fine puppet," he said to
himself. He pulled out his
tools and began to work, but
as he lifted his sharp axe to
cut away the bark, a small
voice suddenly piped up, "Do
not strike me too hard!"

The old carpenter could not
believe his ears. Where did
that voice come from? He
looked under his workbench —
nobody! He looked into the
basket of shavings and sawdust
— nobody! Who could it be?

"I must be getting old!" decided Master Geppetto, scratching his head, and he set to work again. But as his axe struck the piece of wood, the small voice cried out once more, "Ooh, that hurt!"

Master Geppetto was a sight to behold! His hair stood on end, his eyes started out on stalks and his mouth gaped like a fish. It surely could not be the piece of wood talking to him. Why, the log was barely big enough to boil a pan of beans! Shaking his head to try and rid himself of this thought, he picked up his plane and began to polish the wood.

"Stop, stop! You are tickling me!" laughed the voice. But the carpenter simply shook his head again and worked on.

"I shall call my puppet Pinocchio," he decided, as he carved two wooden eyes. But to his astonishment, one eye winked at him. Hurriedly, the old man carried on with the nose — but it wouldn't stop growing. The more he cut it, the longer it grew! As he worked on the mouth the puppet began to giggle and then when the

lips were quite finished the naughty puppet rudely stuck out his tongue!

Geppetto was determined not to give up and he pressed on with the puppet's body, legs, and arms, but no sooner had he done so than the puppet snatched the wig from his bald head and put it on top of his own wooden curls!

How Geppetto raged. "You are a bad boy and should show more respect to your father!" he shouted, but the little wooden puppet jumped off the table and ran straight out of the door.

The old man limped after him but he was no match for the nimble little puppet and soon Pinocchio was out of sight.

"Stop him, stop him!" shouted Geppetto but the watching crowd only laughed as the little wooden puppet raced by. The old carpenter hobbled after him, muttering threats as to what he would do with the puppet once he had caught him, but all at once the chase was over for Pinocchio ran headlong into the arms of a strong policeman! He wriggled and squirmed as the crowd gathered round.

13

"Give him to me," gasped the breathless carpenter. "I'll show him who is master!" But the crowd scolded him and told the policeman to free the puppet for Geppetto would surely beat him once he got home. "We can't be having that!" declared the policeman and he promptly arrested the old man and marched him off to jail.

The sun was fast disappearing over the horizon as the little puppet sadly returned to the empty room. Now he was all alone. "I will run away in the morning," decided Pinocchio.

All of a sudden he heard a strange chirruping. There upon the wall was a big cricket. "Woe betide those naughty boys who disobey their parents and run away from home," he said, shaking his head. "They will never come to any good. Good boys do as they are told and attend school, for if they do not, they will grow up perfect donkeys."

Pinocchio was furious to hear this piece of sound advice and, as the cricket scuttled for safety, he threw a large wooden mallet after it.

Now Pinocchio was tired and
hungry but could find nothing
to eat. Gloomily, he sat before
the fire and soon fell fast
asleep. But his feet were too
close to the embers and, as he
dozed, little by little the wood
burned away. He was woken
by the sound of his father's
voice calling him from the street
but when he tried to run to
the door he fell flat on his face.
Pinocchio's feet were cinders!

Geppetto looked in at the
window and, seeing the poor
puppet lying helpless on the
floor, he soon climbed inside.

17

How he hugged his little
Pinocchio when he saw what
had happened! Sitting the
puppet upon his workbench to
watch, he quickly made him a
new pair of feet, even better
and stronger than before and
soon Pinocchio could run
around faster than ever.

"Now I will make you some
clothes so you can go to school
like a proper schoolboy," said
Geppetto.

Pinocchio nodded his head
happily. He promised he would
be a good boy and do just as
his father wished.

"But I need a spelling book, papa," he said. The good-hearted carpenter went straight out and sold his coat and with the money bought Pinocchio a book, for he was determined to help his son all he could. And so it was that the next day, dressed in his new clothes and carrying his spelling book, little Pinocchio set off down the road for school. Excitedly he thought about all the interesting things he would learn and how the first thing that he would buy with the money he would earn from the job he would get with the knowledge he had learned would be a fine coat with pearl buttons for his father.

Suddenly a waft of music reached him. It sounded so beautiful and tempting that Pinocchio quite forgot his promises to his father and decided he would begin school tomorrow. "I will follow the music today!" he said happily.

When he got to the square where the music was playing he saw a wonderful puppet theatre. The large crowd of children told him that he could watch if he had two pennies but poor

Pinocchio had no money at all.
In vain he tried to sell his clothes
for everyone just laughed at
him. Then he looked down at
the brand new spelling book
in his hand.

"Who will give me two pennies
for this fine book?" he cried and
soon the deal was done with
scarcely a thought for poor
Geppetto sitting at home all
alone and shivering in his shirt
sleeves. Slowly Pinocchio walked
inside the puppet theatre.

There upon the stage were two
beautiful puppets, Harlequin
and Punchinello.

24

As soon as they caught sight
of Pinocchio standing at the
back of the audience, the
excited puppets broke off
what they were saying and
called him onto the stage.

"Here is our brother, Pinocchio!
Welcome, dear brother!" and
with great hugs they embraced
him until the audience grew
quite impatient and called for
the play to continue. But the
puppets were so carried away
that they ignored the people.
The audience stamped their
feet and soon the puppet master
himself strode onto the stage.

"Why are you creating such a disturbance in my theatre?" he shouted at the trembling Pinocchio. He was a huge man and ugly enough to frighten an ogre. His beard was as black as ink and trailed upon the ground. His mouth was as big as an oven and his eyes were like two lanterns of red glass.

He carried a long leather whip which he held high in the air and cracked loudly close by the trembling puppets.

Poor Pinocchio fell to his knees. "Please forgive me!" he begged. "I did not mean to stop the show." And the showman, who under all his bluff and fierce exterior had a gentle heart, was quite moved by the downcast little fellow and allowed the happy puppets to sing and dance the night away upon the stage.

In the morning the showman called for Pinocchio and asked

him about his parents.

"My father is Geppetto, the old carpenter," replied Pinocchio, "and he is quite penniless. Why, only yesterday he sold his only coat to buy me a spelling book so I could go to school." The showman was touched by this tale of generosity and gave the little puppet a gift of five gold pieces to take home to his father.

The puppet was overcome by such a wonderful present and saying goodbye to all his puppet brothers and sisters, he was soon on his way.

He had not gone far when he met a lame Fox and a blind Cat. Slowly they hobbled along the road, the Fox leaning on the Cat and the Cat being led by the Fox.

"I am going home to help my papa," the little puppet told them excitedly. "See here. I have five gold pieces and now papa will be a fine gentlemen and I can go to school!"

At the sight of the gold coins, the Fox stretched out his 'lame' paw and the Cat could not help but quickly peep with her two 'blind' green eyes.

"You do not want to go to school, my young friend," said the Fox. "Through my passion for learning I lost a leg."

"And I my eyes," added the Cat.

"No, no," continued the Fox. "You come along with us to the Field of Miracles and there, if you bury your money, a bush will grow covered in gold coins. You will double your money, triple your money — you will soon have a fortune!"

Up in the tree overhanging the road perched a bird.

"Do not listen to them, Pinocchio!" she squawked.

"Do not take the advice of bad companions!" but with a great leap, the Cat sprung upon her and ate her in one mouthful, feathers and all.

Poor Pinocchio was a bit taken aback by such a show of bad temper but he was indeed tempted by the Fox's offer. Five gold coins were good enough, but a fortune was even better. Soon he had decided to go with them.

All day they walked until at last, tired and hungry, they arrived at the Inn of the Red Crawfish. After ordering and eating a huge meal, the Fox and Cat were shown to one bedroom and little Pinocchio was shown to another. No sooner had he crawled into bed than he fell asleep and began to dream of gold coins.

But when he awoke very early next morning he was most astonished to find his two new friends had already left, leaving him to pay the bill.

"They will meet you at the Field of Miracles," the innkeeper told him, pocketing the money with a sly smile, and so poor Pinocchio continued on his way with dreams of a fortune still playing around his head.

The sun was rising over the horizon when he suddenly heard a small chirruping sound. It was the cricket from Geppetto's workshop sitting

on a branch above the
puppet's head.

"Go back," he called. "Take
your four sovereigns and
return to your father who sits
at home weeping."

"But by tomorrow my father
will be a rich gentleman,"
replied Pinocchio.

The cricket shook his head
sadly. "Don't trust those who
promise to make you rich in a
day. They are either mad or
rogues! The road ahead is
dangerous and you run the risk
of being attacked. Listen to me
and go back!"

But stubborn Pinocchio
would not be dissuaded and he
continued on his way. He had
not gone far when he heard
the rustle of leaves behind
him. There in the gloom were
two evil-looking figures wrapped
in coal-black sacks. They ran
after him on tiptoe and, in a
panic, Pinocchio hid his gold
coins under his tongue.

"Your money or your life!"
hissed the robbers, but Pinocchio
simply bowed low and mimed
that he had no money at all.
When the puppet refused to
open his mouth the bandits

guessed where he had hidden
his money and soon a horrible
fight broke out. Pinocchio
fought tooth and nail and the
animals fought back with sharp
claws and sharper teeth until
finally the strong little puppet
broke free and ran for it. Up
the nearest tree he went, hand
over hand and was soon
perched safe and sound in the
branches high above. But not
for long. As the smell of smoke
and crackle of twigs reached
him, he realised they had lit a
fire and soon his luck would
run out!

In the distance he could see
a small white house standing
out clearly amongst the dark
green leaves of a wood. If he
could only get help there he
might be saved. Summoning up
all his strength, he leapt from
the tree, right over the heads
of the robbers busily feeding
the fire below. Like the wind
he ran over fields and through
vineyards. But the two animals
were even faster and had soon
caught up with him. Roughly
they tied a rope around his
feet and suspended him upside
down from a tall tree. There

he swung slowly to and fro
just like a pendulum.

"Now we will leave you until
you decide you want to open
your mouth," said the cruel
animals and away they went,
laughing heartily.

Poor Pinocchio. A brisk north wind began to blow and he was flung wildly from side to side until his head quite ached, but still he would not open his mouth.

Not far away stood the little cottage. Soon a window opened and a beautiful girl with blue hair and perfectly white skin leaned out. She was a Fairy who had lived in the wood for over a thousand years. When she saw the poor puppet dangling from the tree she sent her Falcon and Poodle to rescue him. The Falcon's sharp beak

cut through the rope and the
Poodle gently laid him in a
beautiful little carriage and
brought him back to safety.

The Fairy nursed him back to
health herself and soon he was
strong and well once again.
Tearfully he related all that had
happened to him since he left
his dear father.

"And the four pieces of gold,
where are they now?" asked
the Fairy.

"I have lost them," Pinocchio
quickly replied, but he was
telling a lie for he had them in
his pocket all the time.

Suddenly, to his great dismay,
his nose grew at least an inch
longer.

"And where did you lose them?"
asked the Fairy.

"In the wood nearby," fibbed
Pinocchio, and his nose grew
even longer.

"Oh, well we shall find them
easily," replied the Fairy.

"Oh, now I remember," said
Pinocchio hastily. "I swallowed
them; yes, that's right, I
swallowed them."

Then his nose grew so long
that poor Pinocchio could
hardly move his head.

If he turned to the right he struck his nose against the bed or the window; if he turned to the left he struck it against the walls or the door; and if he raised his head, he ran the risk of sticking it into one of the Fairy's eyes!

The Fairy looked at him and laughed. "You have been telling me lies, naughty Pinocchio," she said.

"How could you tell?" he said, much ashamed, and the Fairy explained that each time he told a lie his nose would grow a little longer. Then Pinocchio burst into loud sobs, but the Fairy let him cry for a good half hour to teach him a lesson.

Then she clapped her hands and called a flock of woodpeckers. They perched on his nose and had soon pecked it back to its usual length.

51

The kind Fairy kissed him and dried his tears. "Dear Pinocchio," she said. "If you can show me that you can be a good puppet and do as you are told then I will turn you into a real boy." How the little wooden face shone at the thought of that! He would love to be a proper boy.

"But I wish I could see my dear father," he sighed. Then the Fairy smiled and told him that she had sent a message to him and he would arrive at her house that very night. Little Pinocchio was overjoyed and set off running down the road to meet old Geppetto.

But as he ran through the wood who should he see but the Fox and the Cat. He did not recognise them as the bad robbers and so called "Hello!" in a friendly fashion. But they seemed cross and wanted to know why he had not gone and buried his four sovereigns in the Field of Miracles.

"You must come with us now and delay no longer for tomorrow the field will be sold and the new owner has strictly forbidden the burying and doubling of money."

Then Pinocchio was afraid that this might be his last chance to increase his small fortune and with a toss of his head and quite forgetting the cricket and the Fairy's good advice he set off with the Fox and the Cat. After walking for half a day the Fox and the Cat suddenly stopped.

"Here we are," they announced, pointing to a drab-looking field over a ditch.

"*This* is the Field of Miracles?" asked Pinocchio, much surprised for he had expected something altogether different.

But the wily animals persuaded him that if he buried his four sovereigns, watered them well and went away for twenty minutes, on his return he would be rewarded with a fine bush dripping with glittering coins.

So the innocent puppet did all that he was told and after an impatient twenty minutes, returned, eager to see his riches. But to his great dismay when he walked into the field there was no bush to be seen. Where was his fortune of gold coins now? High above, a parrot perched on a branch and watched him.

As he bent to look at the ground where he had buried his coins, the parrot burst out laughing. Angrily, Pinocchio wheeled around. "Who are you laughing at?" he demanded.

"I am laughing at all those simple folk who believe that money grows on trees," said the bird. "I believed it once myself but now I have learnt that the way to earn money is by the work of your own hands or the cleverness of your own brain."

Pinocchio began to tremble at the thought that the tree of gold might have been a trick.

"Those villains, the Fox and the Cat, have fled with your money. You will never see it again," explained the parrot, as poor Pinocchio dug desperately at the bare earth. And it was true — the money had gone.

Then Pinocchio decided to return to the little white cottage, where his dear father might be waiting still.

Wearily he trudged along the road and as dawn broke in pale pink streaks along the horizon, the hungry puppet could see vineyards full of lush purple grapes hanging nearby. Without a second thought, he jumped into the field and reached for the nearest bunch, but just as his wooden fingers brushed the fruit, a heavy hand fell on his shoulder. It was the farmer, and loudly he shouted at the thief and pilferer who should dare to steal his crop.

"You will work for me now, as punishment," he decided and so saying, he led Pinocchio to a dog kennel and chained him up. And there poor Pinocchio stayed for week after week, guarding the farmer's chickens from the stealthy polecats that crept around their run at night.

At last the farmer took pity on the unhappy puppet and setting him free, warned him never to steal again. Pinocchio hurriedly nodded in agreement and set off without so much as a backward look.

But when he arrived back at the Fairy's house there was no-one to be seen. No Fairy and no father. A solitary pigeon told him that his broken-hearted father had given up waiting for his long-lost son and had decided to make a small boat and travel to distant countries in search of his boy.

"Oh, if only I had your wings I could fly to him," cried Pinocchio. Then the kindly pigeon offered him a lift and soon they were soaring high enough to touch the clouds.

Before long they spied a large crowd gathered on the seashore. Swooping down from the sky, the pigeon deposited a grateful Pinocchio on the sand.

"What has happened?" he asked an old woman.

"Some poor man has just set off to look for his son but the sea is tempestuous and the little boat is in danger of sinking."

Pinocchio stood on tiptoes and squinted out to sea. It was indeed his own dear papa and as he watched in horror a huge wave buffeted the small boat and it capsized and disappeared from view.

The crowd groaned but little Pinocchio did not delay. With an anguished cry he jumped into the water and struck out from the shore.

But he had not bargained for the weather. The rain came down in torrents and the waves, racing and tumbling over each other, knocked him about as if

he was a wisp of straw. Soon land was far behind him, his father's boat was nowhere to be seen and he was surrounded by mountainous seas. At last an enormous crest lifted him up with such fury that he was thrown from the water and onto a sandy beach.

With every last ounce of his strength he dragged himself to his feet and set off in search of food and a drink of water. Before long he met a kind-looking lady carrying two large cans of water. But she would not let him sip the water until he had helped carry the cans to her house. How the puppet huffed and chuffed at the thought of having to help, but eventually he reluctantly agreed. The lady then let him drink and eat, and as he finished the last morsel he looked up and was astonished to see that the kind lady was indeed his good Fairy! He threw his little wooden arms around her neck and began to cry bitterly.

"I promise that from this day on I will change my life and be a good puppet and go to school!" cried the remorseful puppet.

"And I will keep my promise,"
replied the Fairy. "If you go to
school and do as you are told,
then I will turn you into a little
boy. It all depends on you!"

And so the very next day
Pinocchio began school. His
best friend was a boy called
Candlewick, for he was as thin,
straight and bright as the new
wick on a little night light. Now
Candlewick was the laziest and
naughtiest boy in the school,
and one day he told Pinocchio
that he had made a plan. He was
going to run away from school
to the Land of Boobies.

"There are no schools there," he told the little puppet, who listened with round eyes. "No masters and no books. That is the place for me! You must come with me, Pinocchio! You would love it too, but hurry for the coach will soon be here to collect us."

Pinocchio quickly shook his head. "No, no, I promised the Fairy I would become a good sensible student. I will stay here," but his voice shook as he said it and the more Candlewick described this wonderful new land where the boys and girls played all day long, the more Pinocchio was tempted to join him in the Land of Boobies.

Soon they could see the coach coming and to his surprise, the puppet noticed it was drawn not by horses but by donkeys. The coachman's eyes sparkled and he spoke to them kindly as he opened the carriage door. It was full of laughing boys and girls all piled high upon one another like sardines in a tin. But nobody grumbled and their eyes shone in anticipation of a land without school!

"Come with us!" they cried.

"But what will my good Fairy say?" quavered Pinocchio, with one foot upon the step. Then, almost before he realised he had done it, he was squashed in amongst them all and they were off!

After driving all through the night they reached the Land of Boobies. Sure enough, the streets were full of children shouting merrily. Some played with balls, some rode wooden horses. Some played hide and seek, others trundled hoops. All were happy and smiling.

Soon Pinocchio and Candlewick had joined the merry throng and were having the time of their lives. Days turned into weeks and weeks into months but one day Pinocchio woke to discover the most terrible thing had happened during the night!

As Pinocchio bent over the washstand he saw reflected in the water an enormous pair of donkey's ears! How he shouted! Soon his neighbour arrived.

"You have donkey fever," she sighed, "and there is nothing you can do to prevent it. All boys and girls who are lazy and refuse to do their lessons will in time become donkeys."

Pinocchio sobbed in despair. "Oh, I should never have listened to Candlewick. I should have returned home to the Fairy, like a good boy."

Just then there was a scuffle

at the door and in burst Candlewick. But a Candlewick with donkey ears! As each guffawed with laughter at the sight of the other they began to run around the room on their hands and feet and as they ran, their hands became hoofs, their faces lengthened into muzzles and their backs became covered with hair! Then, the most humiliating moment of all; they each grew a tail! How they wept! But the only sound they could make was a loud "Ee-aw! Ee-aw!" and their braying soon brought the coachman running.

He took them to market and there they were sold to the highest bidders. Poor Candlewick was led off by a peasant and never seen again, whilst Pinocchio was bought by the owner of a small circus.

Now the real work began. He was fed on hay and water and trained hard every day until he could jump through hoops and stand on his hind legs and dance. How he wished he was back at school and studying hard!

Finally he was ready for his first performance but to the ringmaster's great anger, the poor donkey tripped as he jumped through the hoop and injured his leg. Now he was no use to the circus and soon found himself for sale once again. This time he was bought by a man who intended to skin him and make a drum of him! Poor Pinocchio trembled as the man led him down the path towards the sea. There the peasant tied a bag full of stones around Pinocchio's neck, pushed him into the water and sat down upon a rock to wait until he had drowned.

But the little donkey did not drown! The good Fairy was still looking over him and she sent a shoal of fish who nibbled away at him until they reached the little wooden puppet inside and when the peasant pulled on the string, out jumped

Pinocchio, full of joy to be himself once again. But the peasant was not joyful! He was very angry indeed to have been deceived in this way and so Pinocchio quickly jumped back in the sea and swam strongly away from the man's wildly flailing fists.

Pinocchio headed for the distant shore and was making good work of it when he saw a large blue shape glide through the water beneath him. Suddenly it broke the surface and an enormous whale reared up in front of him!

The whale's mouth gaped as wide as a cave and the terrified puppet could see all the way down his huge throat. Desperately he struck the water with his thin arms but there was no escape and with one gulp, the whale swallowed him down.

Soon he heard a noisy gulping nearby. It was a poor Tunny fish who had been swallowed two days earlier.

"There is no escape," moaned the Tunny. "We must wait here to be digested and that will be the end of us." But Pinocchio was having none of it. He stood shakily to his feet and far away down the other end of the whale's stomach he could see a faint light shining. He walked towards it and imagine his surprise when at last he saw by the faint glow of a candle his dear papa seated at a table!

"Oh, my dear papa! I have found you at last! I will never leave you again!" he cried and they held each other tight as the whale reared and plunged in the sea. Poor Geppetto had been swallowed by the whale, boat and all, as he sank below the waves not far from the shore and now he, too, was waiting to be digested.

"But we must escape!" cried Pinocchio. Taking Geppetto by the arm, the little puppet led the way and soon they were climbing uphill along the animal's slippery throat.

At last they reached his gaping jaws, for the whale always slept with his mouth open. The moon shone brightly as the two contemplated the long drop into the sea before them. Then with a deep breath they clasped hands and jumped.

The sea swirled about them as they made for the distant shoreline but before long the old carpenter was fading fast and Pinocchio knew he would never make it on his own. Then they felt a strong force push them from below and carry them safely on. It was the Tunny fish

who had followed them to safety.
Before long he dropped them
safely on the sand.

And so father and son were
reunited and brought to safety,
and at last it was obvious to
one and all that little Pinocchio
had well and truly learned his
lesson. No more did he
grumble about the work he
was expected to do and before
long he was tumbling from his
bed at daybreak each morning
in order to learn the trade of
basket making. Soon he was
earning enough to care for his
dear father and himself and

could see that there was great satisfaction to be gained from doing an honest job well.

One night he dreamed of the good Fairy. While he slept he thought that she bent over him and said, "Well done, Pinocchio! I will forgive you for all the mistakes you have made in the past. You have now shown that you have a good and willing heart and it is time to fulfil my promise to you."

Just imagine his astonishment on waking to find that he was no longer a wooden puppet but a real boy! Jumping out of bed he found ready and waiting for him a new suit of clothes and a pair of new leather boots that fitted him perfectly. Looking in the mirror he no longer saw the usual reflection of a wooden puppet but instead a cheerful bright-eyed boy with chestnut hair and blue eyes.

He ran into this father's room and there sat Geppetto once again happily working on a beautiful picture frame with his carving tools. Never had Pinocchio seen the old man look so contented and with a merry cry, the boy jumped onto his lap.

"Look, papa," he shouted. "I have become a real live boy and you are happy once again. How could it have happened?" His father held him close.

"It is all your doing, Pinocchio," he said. "When boys who have behaved badly turn over a new leaf and become good, they have the power of bringing content and happiness to their families."

Then Pinocchio laughed aloud. "How ridiculous I was when I was a puppet! And how glad I am that I have become a well-behaved little boy!"

95

CARLO COLLODI

Pinocchio is probably the best known children's book to come out of Italy. Its author, Carlo Lorenzini (1826-90), used the pen-name Carlo Collodi and first wrote the story for a children's magazine where it was published in instalments beginning in 1881. He seemed quite unconcerned about the plot, on occasions only continuing with the story when urged to do so by the magazine's young readers. When it was published as a complete book in 1883 it was immediately popular throughout the world.

Sadly the wild invention and imagination of the original story has been watered down over the years and now the Disney film version of *Pinocchio* is far better known.